Dinosaurs Love Underpants

For Pants-tastic Gabriel ~ CF

For Dave ~ BC

SIMON AND SCHUSTER

First published in Great Britain in 2008 by Simon & Schuster UK Ltd
1st Floor, 222 Gray's Inn Road, London WC1X 8HB
A CBS COMPANY

A CIP catalogue record for this book is available from
the British Library upon request

ISBN: 978 1 84738 209 2 (HB)
ISBN: 978 1 84738 210 8 (PB)

Printed in China

17 19 20 18 16

Dinosaurs Love Underpants

Claire Freedman & Ben Cort

SIMON AND SCHUSTER
London New York Sydney

Dinosaurs were all wiped out,
A long way back in history,
No one knows quite how or why,
Now this book solves the mystery . . .

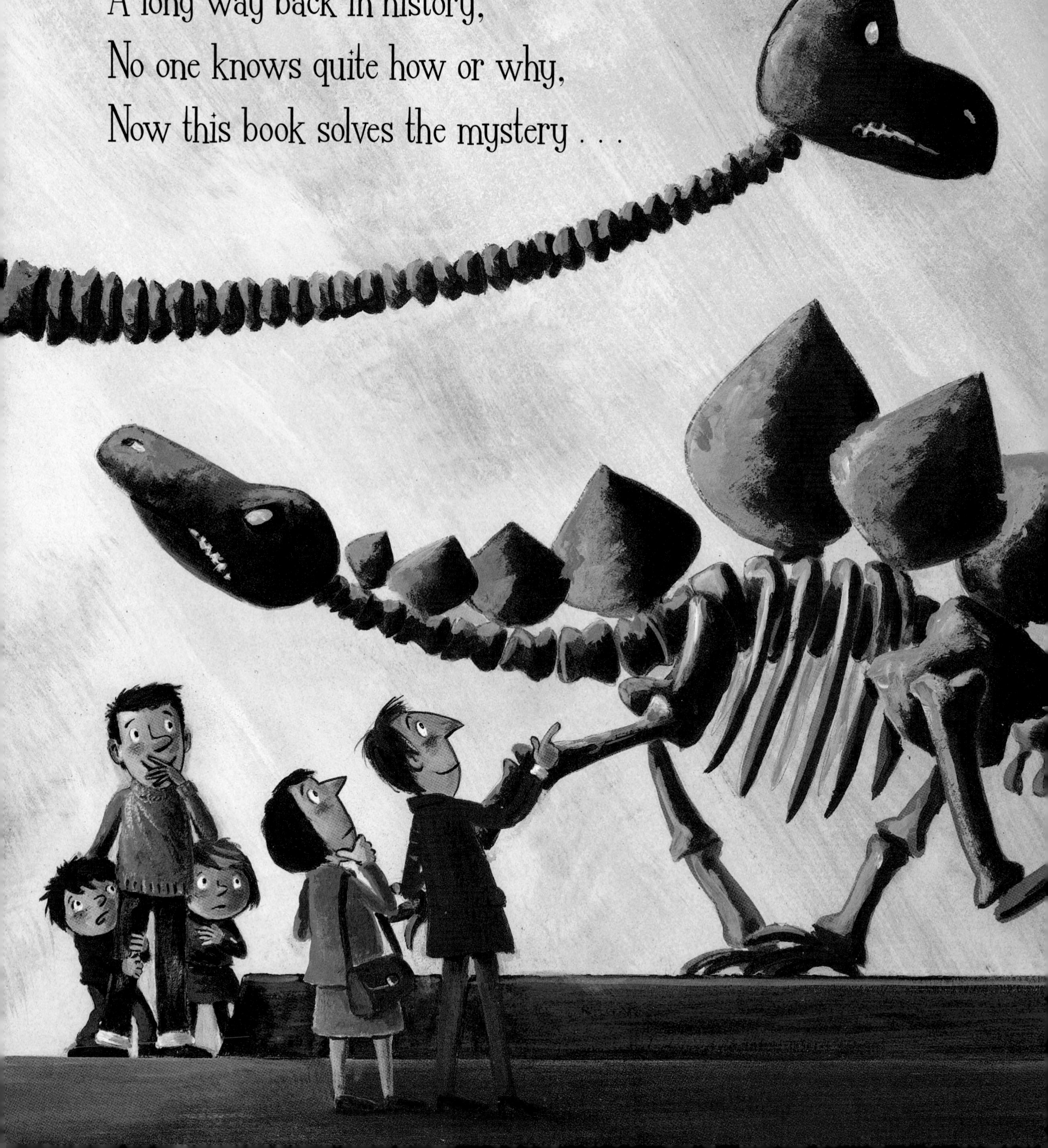

It all began when cavemen,
Felt embarrassed in the nude,
So someone dreamt up underpants,
To stop them looking rude.

The dinosaurs roamed everywhere,
All teeth and huge long necks,
But scariest and meanest,
Was Tyrannosaurus rex!

When T-rex saw Man's knickers,
He roared with deafening rants,
"I don't want to eat you up,
I want your underpants!"

T-rex pinched a furry pair,
But his pants quickly ripped.
He couldn't get them past his feet.
Oh! Whoops! Watch out! He tripped!

Triceratops was happy,
Wearing pants on every horn,
Till Styracosaurus snatched them,
And they ended up all torn.

The pants from Woolly Mammoth coats,
Made Stegosaurus itchy,
Diplodocus was really cross,
His pants were far too titchy!

"We've too few knickers to go around!"
The cavemen quaked in shock,
"These dinos are pants crazy,
They've completely run amok!"

Soon pants were flying everywhere,
All slit by tooth and claw,
The dinosaurs were fighting,
In a great pants tug-of-war.

The Mighty Pants War raged all night,
THUMP, POW, BASH, THWACK, CLOUT!
The fighting got so crazy,
All the dinos were wiped out!

The next day, out the cavemen crept,
And cheered at what they saw,
"Hooray! Our biggest enemy,
Is now at last no more!"

So when you put your pants on,
Always treat them with great care,
Pants and knickers saved Mankind,
They're not just underwear!